S is for Seattle
Copyright ©2015 by Dry Climate Inc.

Printed in Shenzhen, China

First edition

www.dryclimatestudios.com

ISBN
978-1-9424022-8-2

Library of Congress Control Number
2014923026

S is for Seattle

Written by Maria Kernahan
Illustrated by Michael Schafbuch

Our first ones were seaplanes that delivered the mail.

B is for Burke-Gilman,
the trail runs through town.

Built on an old
railroad line,
it sure gets you around.

C is for coffee, it fuels Seattle.

Trivia:
How many
hearts
does an
Octopus
have?

If you get two treats,
we will not tattle.

D is for Dawgs,
UW Huskies are bold.

Root for your team
wearing purple and gold.

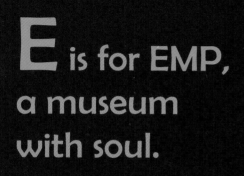

E is for EMP,
a museum
with soul.

Bursting with
pop-culture,
its roots are
rock and roll.

F is for ferries that carry people and cars.

Some make short trips, but others go far.

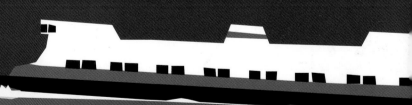

G is for glassblowing
over a hot open flame.

The art that's created
has worldwide acclaim.

H is for houseboats, they are homes that can float.

Perched on the water, right next to your boat!

I is for islands that dot the Northwest.

The view from a seaplane is simply the best.

J is for jerseys of our favorite teams.

Each season we start fresh with championship dreams.

K is for kayaking during busy rush hour.

Glide through the Cut using pure paddle power.

L is for locks that connect the lakes to the Sound.

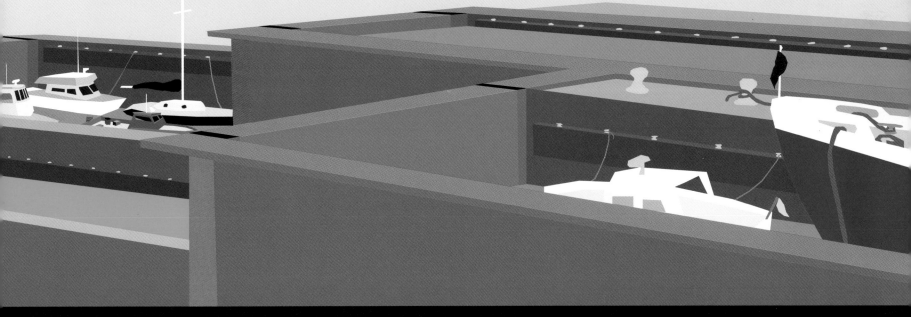

To see salmon swim,
you can watch underground.

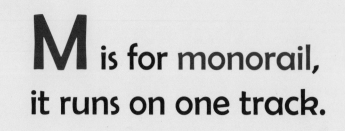

M is for monorail,
it runs on one track.

Hop a ride to the Space Needle...it's fun getting back.

N is for the Native Peoples
who were the first pioneers.

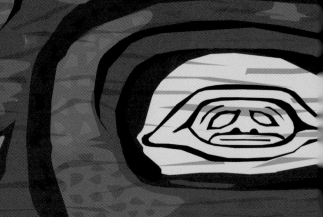

The orca tells the story
of the early Duwamish years.

is for the octopus
that lives deep down in the Sound.

It has three hearts, changes colors
and weighs 600 pounds.

PUBLIC MARKET

P is for
Pike Place Market,
where fish fly every day.

Stop by and do some shopping,
or just hang out and play.

Q is for Queen Anne, one hill of our seven.

Capitol Hill

Renton or Cherry Hill

First Hill

Yesler Hill

Beacon Hill

Each one is unique,
its own slice of heaven.

R is for rain; it's more drizzle than shower.

Just pull on a hoodie — it should last just an hour.

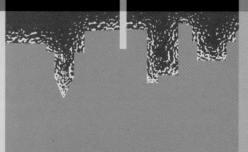

S is for Seattle. It's called the Emerald City.

On a clear summer day there is no place quite as pretty.

T is for the Fremont Troll.
Under a big, dark bridge he sits.

He gobbles up VWs
and other shiny bits.

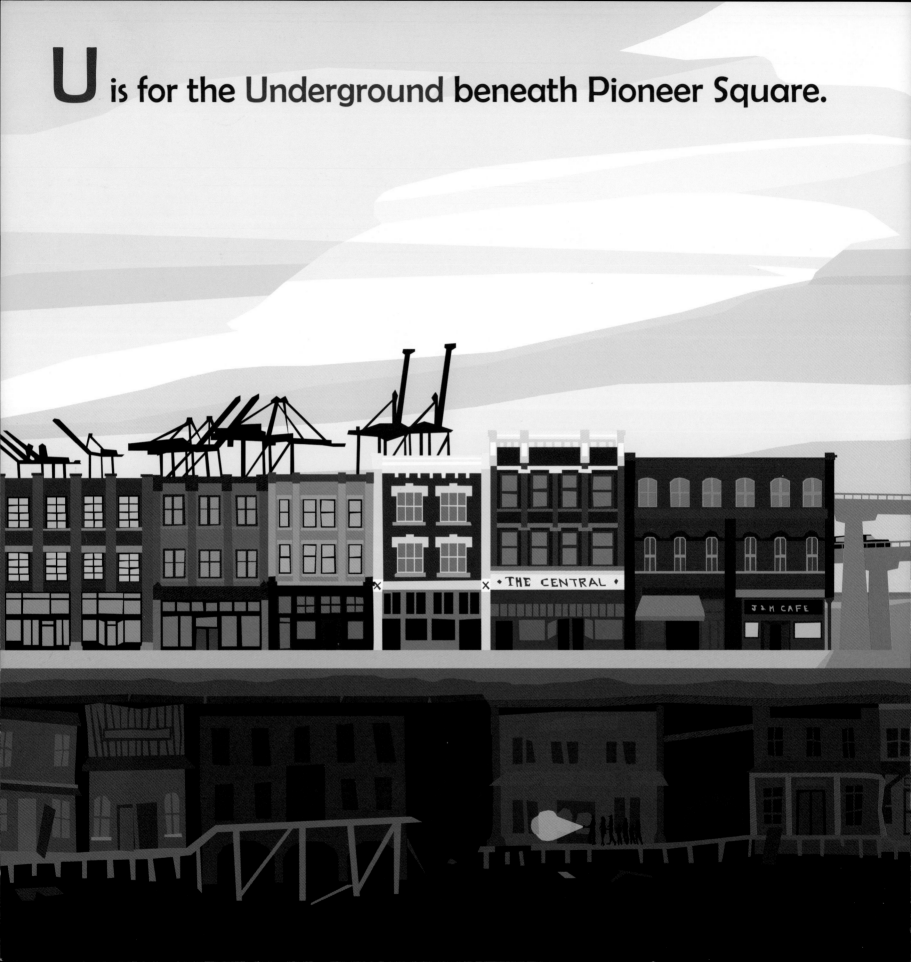

U is for the Underground beneath Pioneer Square.

Visit in the daytime or at midnight if you dare.

V is for volcano.
There's one that we hold dear.

Look up across the skyline —
you can't miss Mount Rainier.

W is for whales. Have you seen the orcas play?

Mothers watch their babies
as they splash around and spray.

X is for the **X**s on the library's glass wall.

A place for books and so much more, it's welcoming to all.

Y is for YUCK! The Gum Wall is gross.
Don't touch it, don't lick it,
but you should see it up close.

Z is for Zzzzzs, that come from someone who's snoring.

Time to get to sleep because tomorrow we're exploring!

WOODLAND PARK ZOO

Thank you

T is for Thank you, it's not just a letter.
Your help was amazing, it made us much better.

Christopher and Matthew, Meggie, Claire and Libby,
Maureen and Big Daddy.

Thanks to the folks who helped us along the way.
We need the extra eyes, big and little!

Joe, Tim and Paul
Tara Magner
Tinker Judson
Duwamish Tribe
Abner Johnson

With inspiration from Troll artists:
Steve Badfanes
Donna Walter
Ross Whitehead
Will Martin

A portion of the proceeds from this book
will be donated to literacy programs in
Seattle through DonorsChoose.org.